ZABURUN

THE DRAGON

WRITTEN & ILLUSTRATED
BY: HARTLY LLOSA

This book belongs to:

____

ISBN-13: 979-8-3570-6549-0

Once upon a time Zaburun was sitting in a field eating lettuce.

Gurtnas, came over from the other side of the field and said, "You are so slow! You are never going to win the dragon race tomorrow! You're probably going to be the first one eliminated."

Zaburun replied, "That's really mean, you shouldn't say that. Anyway, I'm way faster than you. See you at the gym later."

Later at the gym, Zaburun was doing push-ups when Gurtnas burst through the door. He immediately spotted Zaburun and walked over to him and said, "You're going down, man!"

Zaburun replied, "That's not very nice."

"Yeah, that's the point." Gurtnas said, and then he went over to the corner and started lifting weights with his mustache.

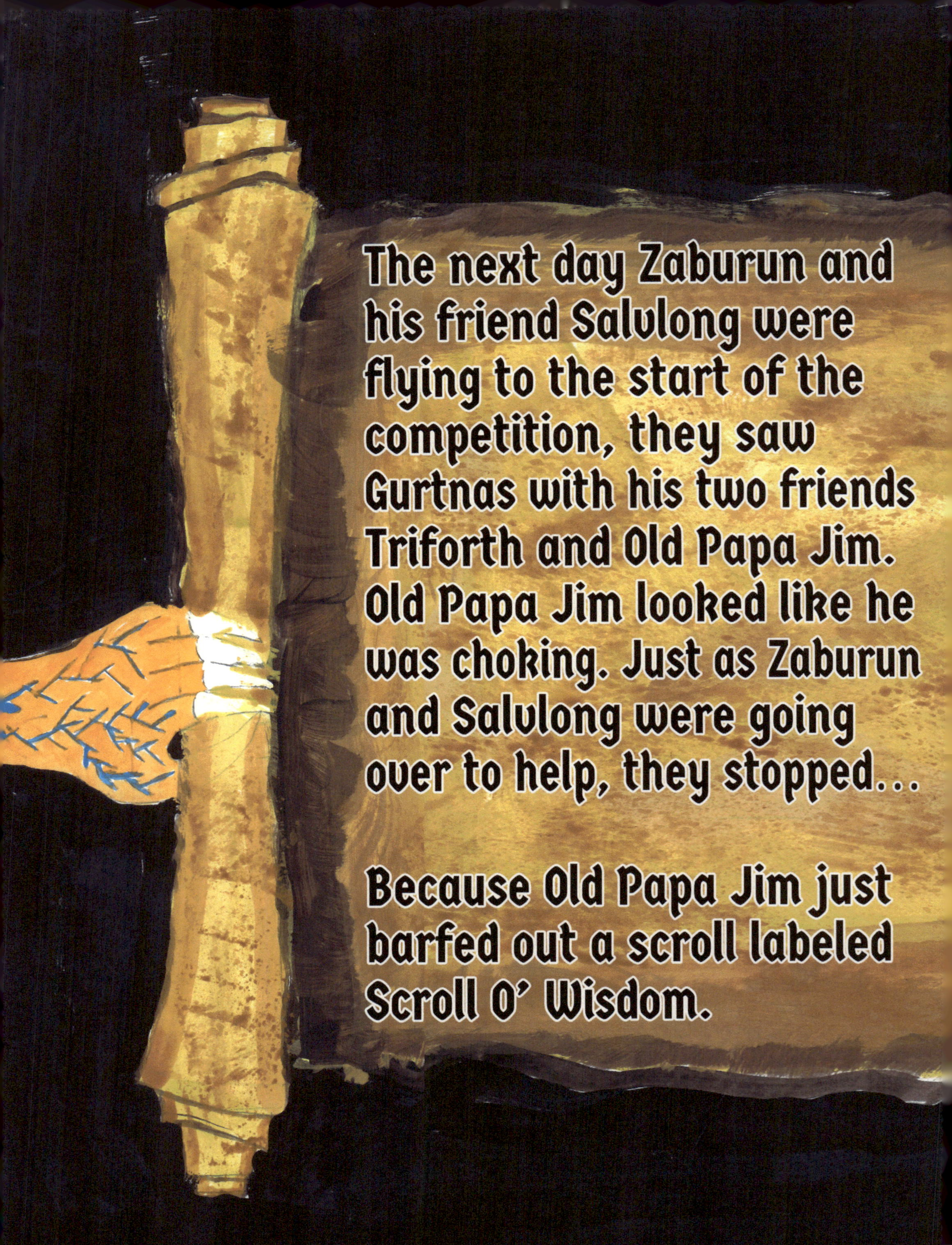

The next day Zaburun and his friend Salvlong were flying to the start of the competition, they saw Gurtnas with his two friends Triforth and Old Papa Jim. Old Papa Jim looked like he was choking. Just as Zaburun and Salvlong were going over to help, they stopped...

Because Old Papa Jim just barfed out a scroll labeled Scroll O' Wisdom.

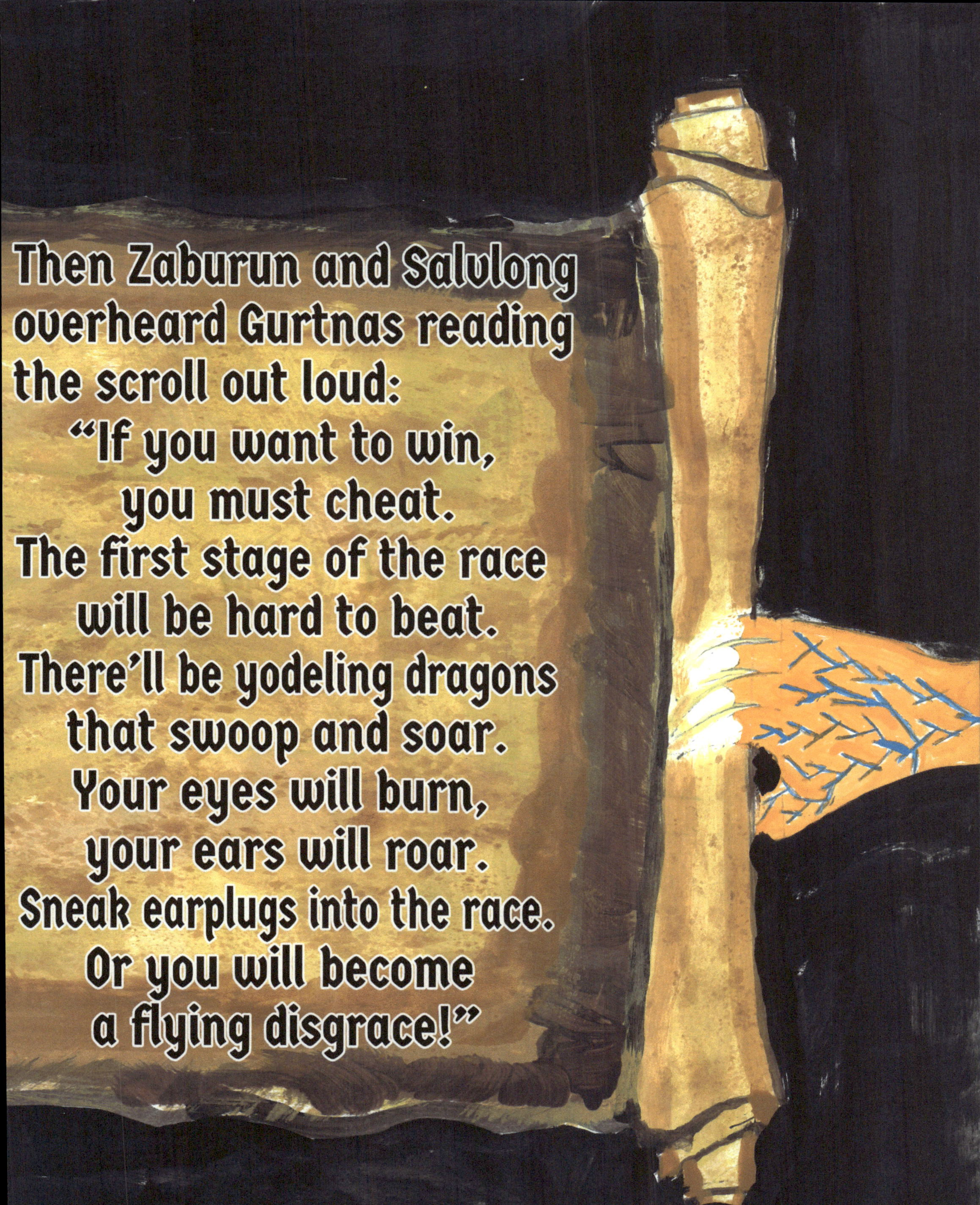

Then Zaburun and Salvlong overheard Gurtnas reading the scroll out loud:
"If you want to win, you must cheat.
The first stage of the race will be hard to beat.
There'll be yodeling dragons that swoop and soar.
Your eyes will burn, your ears will roar.
Sneak earplugs into the race.
Or you will become a flying disgrace!"

As Zaburun and Salvlong went to tell the judge what they just heard, the last call for racers to line up was announced.

The dragons lined up at the top of a volcano and the announcer shouted,

"On your marks! Get set!! GO!!!"

And they were off!

Yodel-a-yodel-a-yodel-a-ee-ee!
Yodel-a-yodel-a-yodel-a-ee-ee!
Yodel-a-yodel-a-yodel-a-ee-ee!

As the racers soared through the air, they saw in front of them a three-headed dragon on a mountain top. Then the mountain dragon mouths opened. Out came a horrible noise:
Yodel-a-yodel-a-yodel-a-ee-ee.

Triforth and two other dragons in the competition dropped out of the sky with their ears smoking.

On the way down Triforth yelled, "I forgot my earplugs!"

Zaburun and Salvong did not have earplugs, but they were able to push through the noise.

As the sound of the yodeling faded into the distance, clouds began gathering and forming into a maze. The four remaining dragons twisted left and right and up and down, then finally three flew out.

Salvlong was not with them, she was still lost in the maze.

Out of nowhere, it started.
Hundreds of meteors showered
the three remaining contestants
(Zaburun, Gurtnas and Old Papa
Jim), they swerved and dodged
the meteors.

Suddenly a meteor hit Old
Papa Jim in the stomach.
Making him barf up another
Scroll O' Wisdom.
As he fell to the ground he
read it:
            You are falling
          from the sky.
       Instead of enjoying pie.
          So maybe start
        flapping your wings.
         What do you think
       of these scroll things?
       Good __   Bad __

Just like that, it was only Zaburun and Gurtnas left in the race. They were closing in on the finish line: The moon. Then out from behind the moon a giant phoenix, a bird made of fire, arose. The phoenix said, "I am Ooglyph. I am the final challenge for this competition, if you can get past me, you will win. Gurtnas swerved left, Zaburun swerved right. But Ooglyph stretched out their wing and batted Gurtnas out of the air.

The finish line was so close, but Zaburun saw that Gurtnas was badly injured from the fire of Ooglyph's wing. Zaburun turned around and went back to help Gurtnas. When Zaburun got to him, Gurtnas looked like he was barely conscious. But then Gurtnas' eyes snapped open, and he pushed Zaburun towards Ooglyph and flew toward the finish line. As Gurtnas was about to cross the finish line, Zaburun flew forward on Ooglyph's back and won the race!

After the awards ceremony, Gurtnas walked over to Zaburun. Zaburun was afraid that Gurtnas was going to be mean to him, but when Gurtnas got to Zaburun he smiled and said, "I'm sorry that I cheated during the race. I just really wanted to win. But using Ooglyph to get across the finish line was brilliant! I can't wait to race against you next year."

And just like that, Zaburun and Gurtnas became friends.

Acknowledgments

Thank you to all the people that helped me make my book, including Dr. Rachel Terlop, Eden Cornelius, Rosebelle & Frank LLosa, and Robert Barnett.

Thank you to all the people on Kickstarter that supported my book, including Sean Shadmand, Kyle Armour, Hadeel, Chris Prunty, Thokozeni Lipato, David Worrell, Blanc Swan, Michael Whittford, Abby Kelly, Meagan McHugh, Holly van Gulden, Ladon Christine, Leah Danoff, Erika Dayton, Stephanie Wang, Holly Hazard, Hope Green Books, Debra Austin, and Katie Brebbia.

Zaburun the Dragon Word Search

```
Z O U R G S N N M C J Z M D Z
M B O Z B U A E V W A N P Z F
E P V G R N D H D L M Y J Q Z
M Q L U L I N J T P U J E R Q
Y W B V E Y O G H R W O F S N
W A R V U Q P J A E O K Z G O
Z Z A R R M S H R H M F N P U
X L Y J W S U A T H I N I N L
M I J A P A P D L O R E F R K
K D E H C N G O Y V L R G M T
D R A G O N Y C Z K L V T C X
S C R O L L O W I S D O M G Z
F Q P I Z G E O J S M M N X M
L A Z W W Q N J R D V S O G F
I Q F O C D L Y C H J J X S N
```

Zaburun, Dragon, Medieval, OldPapaJim, Ooglyph, Salvlong, ScrollOWisdom, Triforth, Hartly

About the Author

This is Hartly's first book, he wrote it at age 12.

When he isn't writing, you can find him reading,

playing D&D with his friends or solving a

Rubik's Cube (his current best is currently 1 min. 3 sec.)

For more information or to contact Harlty,

go to Hartly.com